D1108024

To Vera Braun-Lengyel

Reycraft Books
55 Fifth Avenue
New York, NY 10003

Reycraftbooks.com

Reycraft Books is a trade imprint and trademark of Newmark Learning, LLC.
© HongFei Cultures, 2020
Translation rights arranged through Syllables Agency, France

All rights reserved. No portion of this book may be reproduced, stored in a retrieval system, or transmitted in any form or by any means, electronic, mechanical, photocopying, recording, or otherwise, without written permission from the publisher. For information regarding permission, please contact info@reycraftbooks.com.

Educators and Librarians: Our books may be purchased in bulk for promotional, educational, or business use. Please contact sales@reycraftbooks.com.

This is a work of fiction. Names, characters, places, dialogue, and incidents described either are the product of the author's imagination or are used fictitiously. Any resemblance to actual persons, living or dead, is entirely coincidental.

Sale of this book without a front cover or jacket may be unauthorized. If this book is coverless, it may have been reported to the publisher as "unsold or destroyed" and may have deprived the author and publisher of payment.

Library of Congress Control Number: 2021902282

ISBN: 978-1-4788-7035-7

Manufactured in China

10 9 8 7 6 5 4 3 2 1

First Edition Hardcover published by Reycraft Books 2021.
Reycraft Books and Newmark Learning, LLC, support diversity and the First Amendment, and celebrate the right to read.

Marais, Frédéric, 1965-
The wooden treasure /
2021.
33305249528914
ca   08/19/21

Frédéric Marais

THE WOODEN TREASURE

A long time ago, in a country far away,
there lived a boy who had nothing.

He begged from passersby in the hope of getting a bit of food or some money.

One day, as if out of nowhere, an old man stopped in front of the boy and offered to give him a treasure.

The old man set up several small pieces of wood
and began to explain to the boy how to move them.

The boy, very disappointed, wanted to leave, but the old man began to tell stories as he played with his wooden figurines.

And, in a flash, the boy found himself on a great adventure.

He became defender and conqueror, poor and powerful, soldier and king, victor and vanquished in battle.

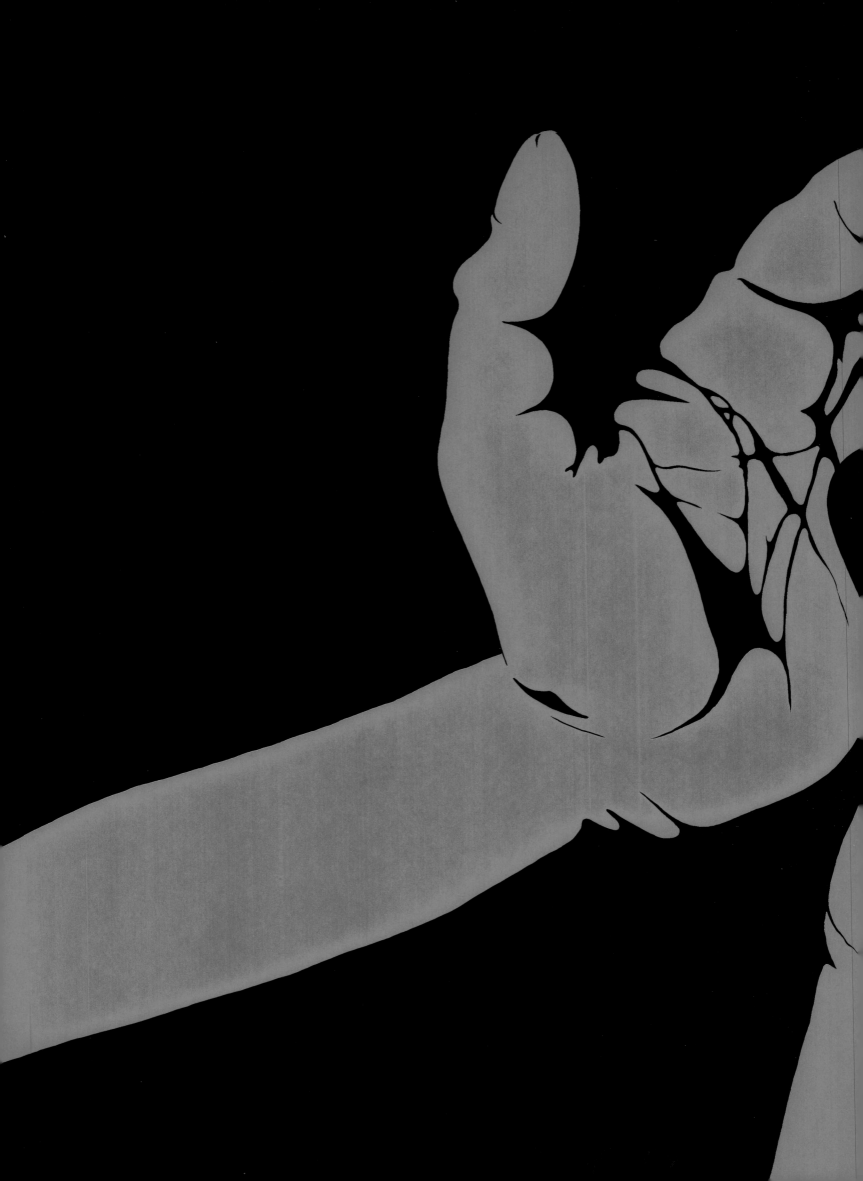

When night fell, the old man offered his wooden
treasure to the boy, then disappeared.

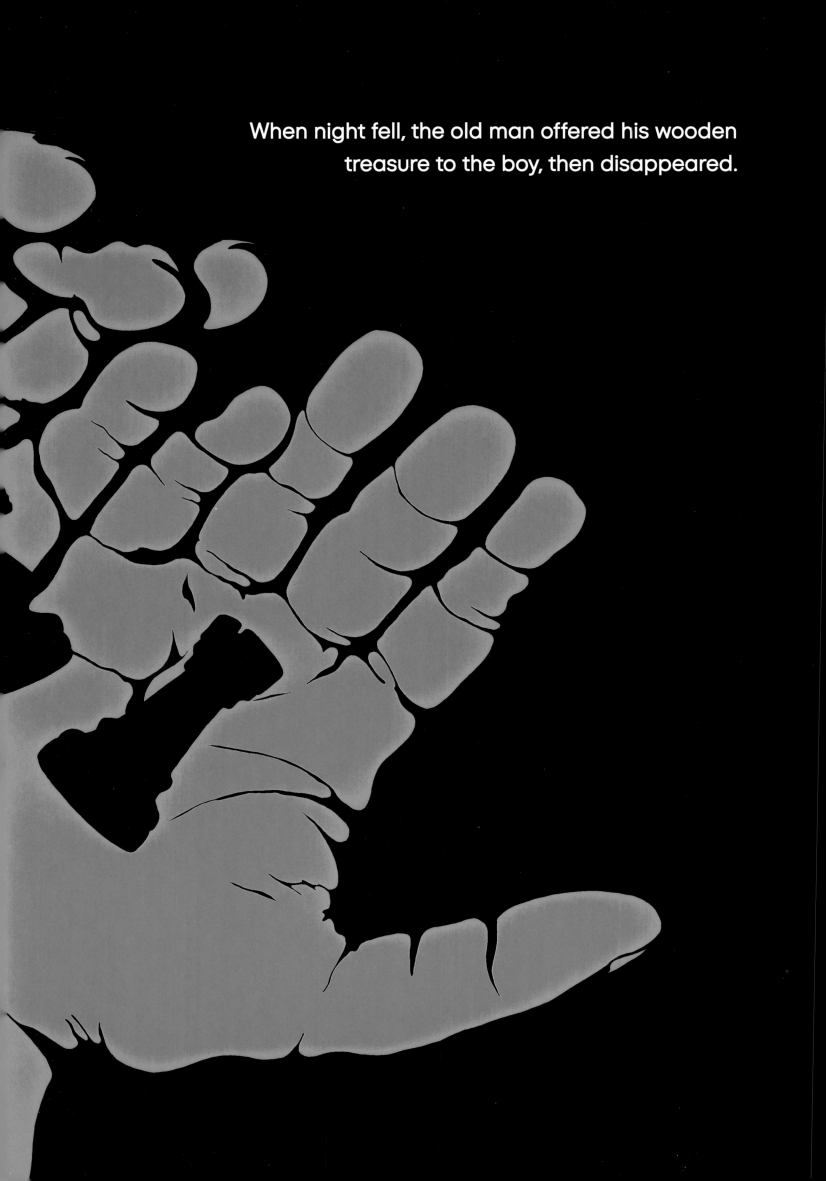

The boy developed a passion for the game and in no time became a player with incredible skills.

His fame reached the ears of a maharajah,
who took the boy under his wing.

The maharajah immediately sent his young prodigy on a long journey so that he could compete against the best players in the world.

The boy played in tournament after tournament, winning them all. He was admired across the globe.

A few years later, the boy returned to his country,
leaving the fame and glory behind.

Time passed.
Then one day he came upon a little girl who had nothing.
He stopped in front of her and, as the old man had done
long ago, offered to give her one of the greatest things
he had ever been given . . . a wooden treasure.

Inspired by the life of Mir Malik Sultan Khan (1905–1966), a gifted Indian chess player who learned to play as a boy and, during his short time playing internationally, was considered the strongest chess master from Asia.

Frédéric Marais is a pupil of the abstract painter Vera Braun-Lengyel. Before becoming an author and illustrator, Marais studied graphic arts and art history and was the artistic director of an advertising agency.